THE GHOST OF CREEPCAT
WITH BONUS CASEY GRIMES STORIES

AJ VANDERHORST   AIDAN VANDERHORST
ASHER VANDERHORST

The Ghost of CreepCat

Copyright © 2021 by AJ Vanderhorst

The Pencil Killer

Copyright © 2021 by Asher Vanderhorst & AJ Vanderhorst

Into Thin Air

Copyright © 2021 by Aidan Vanderhorst & AJ Vanderhorst

All rights reserved.

Published by Lion & Co. Press

No part of this book may be reproduced in any form or by any electronic or mechanical means, including information storage and retrieval systems, without written permission from the author, except for the use of brief quotations in a book review.

www.ajvanderhorst.com

The Ghost of CreepCat (A Sylvan Woods Short Story)/AJ Vanderhorst. - 2nd ed.

CONTENTS

The Books...a Quick Intro	vii
A Warning	ix
The Ghost of CreepCat	1
Note on The Pencil Killer & Into Thin Air	19
The Pencil Killer	20
Into Thin Air	23
About the Authors	27
The End	29

*Dedicated to anyone
who's ever been scared in the woods
and to cats I have known.*

THE BOOKS...A QUICK INTRO

The Mostly Invisible Boy: Casey Grimes 1

Need friends? Try fighting monsters. Casey Grimes thinks his invisibility is permanent until he finds a secret forest society in charge of monster control.

Trickery School: Casey Grimes 2

Classes have begun. Please don't die. Monster-control academy starts for Casey & Gloria, but there's one little problem: A secret enemy who's playing for keeps.

Crooked Castle: Casey Grimes 2.5

Don't mind the dragon. When Brook is dumped on an island by a beast that shouldn't exist, she is haunted by a past that stays just out of reach.

Twisting Trails: Casey Grimes 3

Something's moving in the woods. Casey and Gloria finally have a chance to carve out a home in Sylvan Woods. But something is terribly wrong with the forest itself.

Dark Sky's Ashes: Casey Grimes 3.5

Let sleeping dragons lie. When Conley leaves his safety-obsessed neighborhood, he gets an ancient house with a secret that might roast him alive.

A Warning

BEWARE...this story comes with a warning.

Here it is: *Whatever you do, don't read this one first.*

You may be tempted to ignore our suggested reading order and grab *CreepCat* because it's a quick read. *But that would be a mistake.*

I strongly encourage you—no, I urge you—no, I beg you—read *The Mostly Invisible Boy* first.

The *Ghost of CreepCat* contains a central, solvable mystery and a joke. But...if you don't solve the mystery, you won't get the joke. And if you don't get the joke, you won't be laughing. And who wants to be scratching their head when everyone else is cracking up?

You want to solve the mystery, right?

You want to get the joke.

So read *The Mostly Invisible Boy* first.

Also, you should be aware (surprisingly close to *beware*) that about three in five people find this story...scary.

- AJ

THE GHOST OF CREEPCAT

It all started when a raccoon ate our cat like barbecue chicken.

My twelfth birthday was on a Saturday, and I was trying to have a good attitude. I'd pulled my cinnamon hair back in a bouncy ponytail, the kind that says, *good attitude*. And I'd put on a fun t-shirt: *Hedgehogs: Why Can't They Just Share the Hedge?* And I was wearing my favorite pair of skinny-but-not-death-grippy jeans.

Since I had no friends to celebrate with, I was looking for our cat, Orangesicle, while I waved a piece of bacon. My plan was to slip it to him before my parents noticed so maybe he'd hang around while I opened presents. Then I could throw balls of wrapping paper at him and watch him shred them in a crazy hissing fit like he was being attacked by monsters.

But Orangesicle wasn't in the house. Not even in his favorite lair, a stack of mostly-shredded moving boxes that smelled like something had died—so I stepped outside. For a few seconds, the summer sun hit my skin and I thought, Hey, this could be a good day. Then I saw him.

Well, I saw what was *left* of him, actually, leaning against the house by the front porch. I ran back inside, squeezing the bacon so hard it greased all my fingers.

"Mom, Orangesicle is dead!" I yelled, and she jumped up with a strange, wild look in her eyes and followed me outside.

When she saw him she gave a little scream, and I felt better about the way my stomach had lurched sideways and folded over on itself. We stood there staring at the pile of bones—mostly bare with scraps of pink meat and pale tendons hanging off like someone had been a little too lazy to gnaw them clean.

A puffy raccoon tail lay nearby, so at least Orangesicle had put up a fight. You didn't want to think about what had happened after that, and I tried not to—but I pictured the raccoon eating an Orangesicle drumstick and licking his little paws.

Maybe Mom was picturing the same thing. I'd never seen her eyes so wide, and she must have seen the look on *my* face, because she put a hand on my arm. I swallowed. She sighed.

Then she pulled out her phone and held it up, *click*. She started tippy-tapping away on the screen—and our moment of sadness was over. The shock in her face drained away as she scanned what she'd written, smiled, and tapped a button. *Bling!* I looked over her shoulder at the photo caption:

Burn in hell, CreepCat! Guess you weren't as tough as you thought! :)

"Wow, Mom," I said. "Don't you know the internet's forever?"

"Who cares?" She giggled. "Can you believe he's finally gone?"

I grinned back at her. "It feels wrong to feel so good—but who cares? I'll get a trash bag!"

Ok, so Orangesicle wasn't a great cat. He was supposed to make me feel better about moving, but the best thing about him was his fur, which (surprise) was orange with shadowy stripes—but you never got to touch it. All his fur did was make him look dangerous and stuck up, like he was better than other cats.

And man, was he whiny. As a cute kitten he fuzzed up and hissed whenever he didn't get his way, which was every five minutes. Then without warning, he became a sulky teenage cat, hiding under tables and chairs to swipe at us when we walked past.

Once he bit my thumb to the bone just because I tried to pet him. As my blood dripped on the floor, he narrowed his eyes, licked his teeth and purred. Another time, when my aunt and uncle visited, we caught him trying to claw his way into their baby's pack 'n play. Let me tell you, that was an awful moment.

It's hard to like a cruel, mean-spirited CreepCat like that.

But we were stuck with him.

We tried to take him back to PetSpectacular and trade him in, but they said they'd stopped carrying his type of cat. "What kind is that?" I said. "Murder cats?"

The checkout lady got a weird look on her face and said it would violate their store policy to take him back, and he probably just needed a little more love—which is when I pounded my fists on the counter and Mom said we'd never shop at PetSucktacular again.

And of course, CreepCat sort of understood what we were trying to do. His yellow eyes gleamed through the slats of his carrier. He hated us even more after that.

Dad started carrying a SuperSoaker around the house at all times. Mom started wearing jeans tucked into snow boots, no skirts, so her ankles were protected. My aunt and uncle stopped visiting.

And I hate to tell you this, but I had a recurring dream where I woke up and wandered through the rooms of our house, and when I realized CreepCat was gone, I started dancing—twirling spins and big leaps like a ballerina, as butterflies swirled around me. Whenever I had that dream, I woke up smiling. (But I never told anyone about it.)

I swear that cat hated us all for trying to give him a good life. And he hated me a little extra because I worked harder to make him like me. *Now* maybe you understand how I could look at his gruesome remains and feel bad for about five seconds.

After that, I felt a ton of respect for the raccoon. I made a face, picked up its tail between my finger and thumb, and said, "Mom, can we make a trophy from the tail of this wonderful, magical animal?"

"Lila Banks, that's gross!" she said.

We both started laughing.

My birthday went well after that. With CreepCat gone, Mom and Dad and I relaxed and enjoyed ourselves. I got a new funny t-shirt—*If You Don't Love Tacos, I'm Nacho Type*—and a smartwatch and a pedicure-pocketknife with a tiny nail polish brush and file and everything.

We took our time with breakfast, kicking our legs under the table. For the first time I started to believe that when classes started at Vintage Woods Middle School, I'd fit in and be able to make friends.

Wow, having that cat gone made everything better.

Mom disappeared and returned a little later with her hands behind her back.

"Surprise!" she said, and held out one of my old ball caps. A bedraggled raccoon tail swung from the back. "I had to disinfect it first," she said. "But don't worry, it will get nice and puffy again—I think."

I covered my mouth with one hand.

"Wow," Dad said. "It's so..."

"So cute!" I said.

We all started laughing again. The raccoon cap was really awful, but I put it on anyway, because I felt good—and hey, I admired that raccoon.

After lunch Dad and Mom had some things to do, and I decided to take a hike in the woods. Maybe it was the hat's influence. I felt like I was wearing a charm that would bring good luck.

And let me say this, dear reader. I'd better warn you now. The fun, happy part of this story is over. (And remember, you already saw the bones of a dismembered cat.) Because let me tell you, I was very, very wrong.

At first, the woods seemed like just the kind of place you'd want to hike through. The trail looped around roots like muscly arms. Plenty of shade kept me from getting too hot. The air had a fresh, greenish tint, and the trees rocketed up like they wanted to reach the sun, big explosions of leaves splashing the sky.

I hoped I'd get a look at the raccoon, moving slowly after his huge dinner. I imagined us nodding at each other, and I'd say, "Hey bud, thanks for saving my birthday—and my ankles. That cat was a demon."

And he'd say, "For a demon, that thing sure tasted good."

And I'd say, "I hope you don't mind this hat—it's in your honor."

And he'd say, "You got it, girl. That tail looks way better on you than it did on me, although I miss it."

And I'd say, "Hey, I know you're wild and all, but we've got, well, some vacancy at my house in case you'd ever wanta–"

"Of course I'll hang out with you sometimes," he'd say. "You cool." Then we'd throw each other a peace sign and he'd fade into the shadows, my raccoon friend. And as he scampered off, I'd say–

Rawr!

I froze in the trail with my mouth half open. As I turned, the tight hairs at the back of my ponytail tugged my skin.

Orangesicle crouched in the middle of the trail with one paw shading his eyes. He'd never liked the sun very much, and seeing him there in the open, not sulking and slinking around the house, I realized how *big* he'd got before the raccoon ate him.

He shot his claws out—*shnick*—squinted his eyes half-shut, and started stalking me through the shade. His jaws gaped open in a slowly widening grin.

Betcha didn't know my mouth could get this big.

Oh no, I thought. Oh no oh no.

You know the feeling you get when something horrible happens that, in a thousand years, you never would've seen coming, even though you can think of all kinds of bad things that could happen?

Well, maybe you don't. But my chest got replaced by this sharp, shaking, silent scream. My heart and lungs and brain did somersaults in a dark, cold place. Then I trembled all over and backed away from the ghost of CreepCat.

"You're not real," I whispered. "You're dead. I'm not really here."

Of course I *was* really there—I got that part wrong

because I was panicking. I was in a huge, strange forest: the kind of place where the ghost of my demon cat could come get me. And he'd probably heard me talking about him to the raccoon.

The raccoon! As I started running, I thought, If-I-can-just, *gasp*, find-my-friend, *gasp*, the-raccoon! And it made total sense. That raccoon had devoured Orangesicle once and he could do it again.

So I ran like crazy, and it turned out I was a pretty good runner—even though I was wearing my glittery *good attitude* sneakers. I skidded around curves and shot down every straight piece of trail I saw.

When the path broke up into two or three paths, I always chose the straightest one, so I could sprint faster. And I tried to keep my eyes up, looking for the raccoon, even though it meant I kept tripping.

Once my toes snagged a root, and I *thwapped* the ground like a cardboard cutout and crawled ten feet before I pulled myself up and kept running—because I wasn't gonna start crawling backward, sobbing, like the girls in those horror movies.

But it *was* a horror movie—it really was. The ghost of CreepCat was hunting me through the woods with his jaws unhinged so he could eat me.

I ran for as long as I could. It might've been twenty minutes. It might have been an hour—but I suddenly stopped and bent in half with my hands on my knees, because my lungs had stopped working. Huge, shuddering breaths that were half sobs made me shake all over and I couldn't help it.

Ok, I thought, ok. Now you've got to circle back the way you came.

That's what I started to do, because I'd given up on the

raccoon. He was probably asleep in his den. But I was sure if I could just get out of the woods, CreepCat's ghost would leave me alone.

At first, it worked. I walked as fast as I could, one hand pressing my ribs. With a stitch in my side, I kept gasping for air, but I wouldn't stand still and let Orangesicle catch me.

The trails seemed to lead toward my house, like the forest was trying to help. *Here's a path home, little girl—and another, and another. Your choice, any of them will work.*

And it *would've* worked, except CreepCat wouldn't let me take those paths. Every time I started down one, I'd hear his mocking, hungry yowl ahead of me—with a little slurp on the end as he licked his teeth.

And then the sun started to go down. And the paths stopped trying to help *me*, and they started helping him instead.

All those trails pointing back to Vintage Woods disappeared like they'd changed their minds. *Now* every path I followed curved deeper into the gloom.

Sometimes there'd be a homeward loop, and my heart would do a backflip—*I can do it, I can get back to Dad and Mom and my birthday cake*—and then the trail would swoop around again, like it had been waiting to trick me and make me cry.

I didn't cry though. Not one tear. All the water on my face was sweat, believe me. Every single drop. I mean, it was just darkness. It was just a haunted forest. It was only a ghost cat on my trail.

Ok, so maybe I cried, just a little. But I stopped crying when I realized I couldn't let CreepCat herd me deeper and deeper into the woods. I was probably miles from home and getting further away.

So I flipped my ponytail and felt the raccoon tail brush

the back of my neck, and I thought, *You have to make your own luck*. I pulled my new pocketknife out of my pocket and opened every single tool, even the little brush. Then I put my back to a huge, bumpy tree and waited, trying to make myself stop shaking.

By now the woods were so dark that all I could see were shadowy shapes. Trees looked like giants with twisted fingers. Ferns and bushes looked like hungry hands.

Orangesicle knew I had stopped running. I could hear it in his eager, high-pitched whine. A minute later I saw him coming down the trail. The sun was so far gone, now he looked like what he was: a ghost. His glowing eyes floated over a swirling, stripy shadow.

When he got closer, he slowed to a crawl, and I could see his bristling fur and hear the slurp in his snarl as he stretched his jaws.

"You're—you're just a—just a ghost," I said, trying to keep my voice from shaking. But I didn't do a very good job. If that cat could've talked, he would've said, Oh yeah? You think so, huh Lila? Can a ghost do this?

He launched himself at my neck.

You probably won't believe me, but I hadn't screamed all day until that second.

You've never heard a scream so loud and long and totally unlimited. It just went on and on, flying out across the night, as I did the only thing I could. I swung my fist up and stuck it in CreepCat's mouth as he crashed into me.

I wish I could call it a punch. It was a desperate, awkward shove, and as I fell to the ground, I kept shoving. I jammed my fist into his throat, up to my elbow—and the whole time I kept hearing my scream like it was someone else's voice, flying out over the forest like a radio frequency.

I knew I was about to die, I guess. But deep inside, I'd

thought maybe CreepCat might take my hand as a sacrifice and let me go, and I'd jerk free from his mouth and stumble back home to my parents, holding my bloody wrist, while he crouched over my hand, chewing up my knuckles, *crick-crick-crack*—and swallowing them one by one.

At least, that would've bought me a little time.

But that's not what happened.

I felt his claws dig into my chest and my stomach, his muscles tightening for the big slash that would spill my heart and guts into the dirt. He didn't want just one hand—he wanted all of me. I knew it was the end.

Maybe I'd known all along it would end this way, ever since I'd seen him crouching in the trail behind me and slowly unhinging his jaws.

How did I ever think I'd get away? I was just a girl who put her hair in ponytails and talked to imaginary animals and wore silly, upbeat Ts and hoped for the best when she really shouldn't.

My scream faltered and broke like glass. It ended in a gasping hiccup. My arm was gone. My heart and guts were gone.

Stars rushed toward me through the trees.

I didn't even get to—was my last thought, and I could have ended that thought a hundred different ways, but I didn't have time.

The woods went black. Darkness wrapped itself around me in sheets.

I died.

In death, the night became thick, and hot, and furry. Then the darkness got gross and sticky—and no one can sleep through that.

I woke up.

When you think about it, dying from a monster attack would probably be a lot more painful.

It took me a minute to realize I wasn't dead. CreepCat lay on top of me like he'd finally become a snuggler and was trying to keep me warm. But his claws were hooked in my shirt, pricking my skin like needles, and even if he'd become all touchy-feely, I wanted him off me *right that second*.

So I tried to shove him off, but I couldn't. We were stuck together. My breath caught in my throat and my heart started hammering as I remembered CreepCat had eaten my arm.

I flopped onto my side and he rolled off me. He took my arm with him, which brought tears to my eyes, because now I'd have to go through life lop-sided. But then I winced as my shoulder twisted, and I realized I could feel his fangs digging into my elbow.

"Ow, ow, ow," I breathed. What happened next, to be honest, was a lot more painful and disturbing than the moment when I'd died.

Slowly and stickily, I pulled my hand out of CreepCat's throat. It would've been a lot harder—maybe it would've taken a surgical operation—but one of the blades on my pocketknife, the mini nail-scissors, maybe, had stuck inside his gullet and opened him up like a fish.

You wanna know how gross this was, and how much blood I had on me, by the time it was over?

Well, I won't tell you—except to say that CreepCat's second mouth, the one in his neck, was bigger than his first one, and I thought there were huge worms squirming in his throat—and almost passed out again—until I realized I was looking at my own gooey fingers, slippy-sliding up toward his teeth.

I wriggled my fingers and gave myself a little wave.

It felt like someone else was waving, from inside CreepCat.

Sorry! I might've said too much, but I think maybe that's what happens when you go into shock. To me, can you believe it, it seems like I'm giving you just exactly the right amount of info!

When I got my arm out, I had red grooves running from my elbow to my wrist and several deep gouges where Orangesicle had tried to lock onto me as I'd shoved my fist past his teeth, slicing him open as I went.

I did my best to wipe all the blood on grass and leaves, but I still felt sticky. Then I sat down on a mossy rock and stared at Orangesicle, who had now died twice. My eyes kept sliding back to the big red gap that started under his chin and ran halfway down his chest. If I looked closely, I could actually see pieces of—well, you probably don't need to know that part.

Wonder if I'll have to kill him again, I thought.

And I wrapped my hand tighter around my pocketknife, although I didn't really have to, because it was basically stuck to my palm. The moon rose high over the woods. I felt like the trees were leaning down at me, reaching for me with twisty, pointed fingers, but they hadn't decided whether to pat my head or crush me.

And then the dangerous-looking boy showed up.

Why dangerous-looking, you ask? Well, there were dark circles under his eyes. There was his dark hair, *very* spikily spiked. There were his tight-fitting, army-looking clothes—all of them black. Oh, and also, he was carrying some kind of axe with a wicked blade and a long handle. The axe was black too, obviously. Lots of clues, you see, but I didn't especially care.

I giggled. "Isn't it a little late for chopping wood?"

THE GHOST OF CREEPCAT

The boy looked offended. Then he glanced at the bloody circle I was sitting in, and the ghost of Orangesicle beside me, and he said, "Hmm."

That's it. Hmm. Are you kidding me? I knew I deserved something better than *Hmm*. A funny t-shirt about killing ghosts would've made a lot of sense. A hug—heck yeah I deserved a hug—and a warm blanket and a whole box of bandaids. At the very least, a smile.

I felt a tear drip down my cheek.

The dangerous-looking kid looked uncomfortable, and for some reason that made me feel better, like I had a tiny bit of influence on the situation, so I kept right on crying.

"Ok, ok, ok." The kid put out his hand and kind of hovered it over my shoulder like I was a stove and he was checking the temperature. I grabbed it with my left hand, the one without the pocketknife, and squeezed.

He let me do that for about five seconds, his eyebrows darting toward the moon. Then he carefully unfolded my fingers, hesitated, and patted me on the head. That's right, he *patted me on the head* like I was six years old—and not even that really counted, since I was wearing my coonskin cap.

"I should probably knock you out and take you in for questioning," he said, "but I was wrong *one* time a while back, so I try to keep an open mind. Um..." He bit the inside of his cheek. "Guessing you don't know someone special who used to live in your neighborhood—or two special someones, one big and one little? The smaller one loves glitter glue and unicorns."

When I didn't answer he kept going.

"Well, looks like you did what you had to—but hell's bells, think you could've splashed any more blood around? I mean, I'm not sure there's enough."

I found that pretty insulting. Sure, maybe I looked like I'd been spray-painted red, but I'd killed the ghost of my demon cat, and anyone, absolutely anyone, should've found that impressive. I don't care how much black you wear.

The kid wrapped his hands around the top of his axe. "Here's the deal," he said. "I'm going to take you home. Maybe you were looking for us, maybe not—and if you were, well, you're right, we're out there, but I won't say another word about that. Now let's go."

When I realized he wasn't going to help me up, I got slowly to my feet.

"You're out there?" I said.

"Yeah." He'd already started down the trail.

"Who's out there?" I said. "Some kind of secret forest society?" I gave my best non-shaky laugh.

He frowned at me over his shoulder.

"And what does this secret society *do*?" I said brattily.

He turned with his hands on his hips, somehow still holding the axe. "Look," he said, "this is it. This is the last thing I'm saying, whether you're joking or you're really clueless or what. We do—we do—what you just did to that thing."

"Wait!" I said as I forced my legs to work. "You mean— you mean, you kill horrible, dangerous cats?" It was a weird idea, very weird, and kind of dark, but I have to admit...I liked it. I liked it a lot. What if Orangesicle came back?

"You're funny," the kid said. "Hey. I guess if you're meant to figure it out, you will."

And that was the last thing he said. Seriously. I asked him how I could get in touch if I needed help. I said, "Hey, by the way, my name's Lila Banks, what's yours?" I asked him if he ever lost track of himself in the dark, wearing all that black. I asked him how long he'd been killing horrible cats.

Anything to get him to talk, but he wouldn't. Not a word, not even a smile, until I saw the lemon-white glow of floodlights in my yard and the flashing blue strobes through the trees.

Know what he said to me then?

"Hubba hoy, Lila." He was right beside me when he said it, and when I turned to say, "What the heck is that supposed to mean?" he was gone. Gone without a "Take care, ok?" or a goodbye pat on the head. Gone with a *hubba hoy*.

What a weird, annoying, dangerous kid.

You can imagine what happened when I stepped into my backyard. The whole place was lit up like it was noon. I looked like I was spray painted red, and I was holding a bloody pedicure-pocketknife.

You should've heard Mom scream. Hers was a good one, but it didn't even come close to my scream in the woods.

I told the police the truth: the ghost of our cat, Orangesicle, had lured me into the forest and tried to kill me but I'd killed it instead. They looked at me like I was crazy. One of them shrugged. Another covered his mouth. They told my parents, For God's sake, get this girl to bed. And I thought, Right? About time—thank you!

Mom sponged me off in the bathtub, crying over my cuts. She and Dad brought me birthday cake in bed and they told me, Sure, you can have a funny t-shirt about killing ghosts, but let's not talk about it right now, ok?

I found that really irritating, because *talk about it* was all I wanted to do.

It got even worse. For the next few days, they kept not-wanting-to-talk-about-it, and then I had to go to school.

And here's something weird. That kid—the dangerous, annoying one that I don't like? He was not there, even though I looked everywhere—just to make *sure* he wasn't there. And no one believed my story about the woods.

Of course, I should've known better. Looking back, I shouldn't have told them about my battle with the ghost of my dead cat.

And I really shouldn't have mentioned that somewhere out there in the woods is a secret society. A secret society that I might find my way back to, if it's meant to be.

And I definitely shouldn't have told Tony, who sits next to me in Math, that I sorta like to think I have what it takes to be part of a secret society that fights evil, killer cats.

And I really, definitely, shouldn't have asked him, "What do you think, Tony? Do you think I might have what it takes?"

Because he thought about it for a second. Then he said, "Yeah, Lila. I really, really do. I think you have what it takes."

By the next day, that's what everyone at Vintage Woods Middle School was saying to me. "Hey Lila, hey girl—you have what it takes!"

And that's who I am now. I'm that weird girl who wants to fight killer ghost cats—and everyone tells me I have what it takes.

Mom says, "Let's be honest, honey. You kind of brought this upon yourself."

Dad says, "Look sweetheart, *I* still like you—whatever other people say."

But I *did* follow the ghost of CreepCat into the woods, and I did meet a cool, dangerous-looking kid—I mean, not very cool—but he told me I'd find my way back if it was meant to be, and now not *only* do I not have friends, but I'm really struggling to concentrate on my studies.

But here's the good news: the ghost of Orangesicle hasn't returned.

I think I traumatized him even worse than that raccoon did—and wow, let me tell you, after fighting CreepCat myself, I've got even more respect for that raccoon. He made it look way too easy. One of these days I'm sure I'll run into him, hiking through the woods, and we'll look at each other and *know*.

You're the real deal, girl.

You've got my respect, raccoon.

Peace.

But let me ask you a question.

It's important, so take your time.

And no fake answers please. This isn't a joke.

Somewhere out there in the woods is a secret society with dangerous-looking kids who are maybe sorta-cool, and they fight the ghosts of evil killer cats. And if it's meant to be, I might be able to find them.

But it's not for everyone, that's for sure.

So what do you think?

Be honest, ok.

Do you think I have what it takes?

THANKS FOR READING THE GHOST OF CREEPCAT.

If you're wondering what to read next, it's probably time for a full-length Casey Grimes novel. Learn more at **ajvanderhorst.com**.

For all the inside stuff on the Casey Grimes universe—including a free story, book news, and tips on fighting monsters—sign up for *The Sylvan Spy* at **ajvanderhorst.com/invisible.**

NOTE ON THE PENCIL KILLER & INTO THIN AIR

These stories began as school assignments and we had fun with them anyway. In case you get the wrong idea, the character and setting were totally up for grabs.

Thirteen-year-old Asher and fifteen-year-old Aidan came up with the concepts. AJ pitched in with revisions. We ended up with a couple tales with a twist that create a new angle on someone you may *think* you know from the Casey Grimes books.

(If you haven't read any of the full-length novels, you may want to read one first.)

These stories were originally circulated in *The Sylvan Spy*, an elusive secret message ring.

We hope you enjoy reading these as much as we did writing 'em.

Read at your own risk...

THE PENCIL KILLER

The electric pencil sharpener whirs metallically as it eats a new, orange pencil into a pointed tip. I sigh.

This is my fourth pencil and it's only been fifteen minutes. Today's drawing session isn't going exactly *great*.

I exit the utility room and cross the kitchen. A healthy beam of sun slices across the dining room table through the glass sliding doors that open on our deck. Sitting down for the fourth time, I try to get comfortable, try to get in my creative zone.

But it's really hard.

Scratch-scratch-scratch comes at me from the other side of the table. I grip my pencil tighter and glance at the boy across from me.

Dressed in olive-green camo and khaki, he hunches over his own paper, scribbling away with a rapidly-shortening pencil. But *scribbling* might be an exaggeration.

It's hard to say if he's trying to get a picture down—you know, *capture* it—or trying to injure the page like it personally insulted him. Now and then his face scrunches up, making his freckles dart around.

His left hand grabs at his tousled brown hair as he stabs and jots with his right. Working hard not to stare, I try to get a read on his mood. His bright blue eyes have a look that's hard to describe. Focused but also...wild? Maybe a good word is *dangerous*.

Which probably explains what is happening in this room.

This kid is the reason I am sharpening so many pencils. Wood shavings and eraser peels surround him like sketchy confetti. Sometimes it's the sign of a good artist.

It can also be the sign of a struggling one.

As he jabs away at his drawing, I decide the struggle is real.

"So," I say, looking down at his battered paper. "What's that?"

That appears to be a grey, smudgy cylinder. Pencil lead streaks the page, and I can't decide if it's supposed to be rain or nighttime. I decide either way, it's darkness.

The boy shrugs. "Well, I was *trying* to draw the Big Beech," he says without looking up. "But then I started thinking about the first time I saw a Butcher Beast. It happened in that tree, at the top of the bleachers during a sleepover—and, well, things got out of control fast."

His pencil-tip snaps off, making another rip in the page, and I wince. That was pencil number five. I hope he's not gouging Mom's table.

The boy scratches his head. "Maybe we should go and climb a tree instead of doing this." He looks up, brushing away shreds of eraser.

I consider the dark fate that will befall the rest of my drawing supplies if we continue. Broken pencils scattered everywhere like small dead trees. Crumpled paper littering the table like fallen clouds.

Screams.

Fire.

Death.

Maybe the boy across from me is picturing something similar—but not in an artistic way. My scalp tightens up. The room seems small. It would be great to get out in the sun.

"Climbing sounds good," I say. "I think we've caused enough chaos already"—but of course I mean *you've* caused enough.

I give his badly hurt paper a salute and put a hand on his shoulder like I'm about to give him some advice. A second later I jerk it back, remembering his mood level is dangerous.

"Umm, Casey," I say, "I think it'd be best if you stick to killing Butcher Beasts. They're your real enemy, right? Not paper and pencils."

He laughs. "Good point. So, should we go climb something huge and twisty?"

"Let's do it." We head outdoors, he relaxes, and my head and neck stop tingling.

Casey Grimes is one of the nicest kids you'll ever meet. He looks you right in the eye, pays attention when you talk, and is good at remembering names. But his capacity for destruction is a little scary—especially when he's not even trying.

~

INTO THIN AIR

I t's getting dark as I sit on top of the arbor, our four-posted play structure that stands eleven feet tall.

"He said he'd be here by now," I mutter and drop to the ground, scanning the yard.

No sign of him.

I'm bending down to tie my shoe when...

PHWOOSH! Something zips over my head.

"HEY!" I bellow, "DID SOMEONE JUST TRY TO KILL ME?"

A boy steps out from behind a tree. Wind rustles his spiky hair as he smirks. "Sorry, you kinda looked like a female Bog Creep in this light."

I run my hands through my own hair, kind of floppy and not nearly as spiky as his. Is any of it missing?

"Wow, thanks Robert. Very funny."

I stand a little straighter. A female Bog Creep? Seriously?

He stalks past me and yanks out a sharp, disk-like object imbedded in a tree at the level of my neck.

I shudder. "Ok, you ready to go?"

He snorts. "Of course I am. Question is, are *you*?"

I raise an eyebrow. "Hey, I'm the one who's the pro at this. You're just a first-timer."

We walk over to the tall, wooden structure. Once we've both climbed the ladder, I review important topics, like how to land without dislocating anything, and staying composed as you fall.

But I'm not sure Robert is paying attention. He looks over the edge at the trampoline like he's sizing up an enemy.

"Ok, enough." I give up on my tutorial. "You good to go?"

He nods, climbing onto the narrow wooden rail.

Man, I'm excited to see this. "The first time can be a little scary," I say. "Want me to count down? Three, two—"

He jumps. I can almost swear he has a smirk on his face as he flies into space. Robert does what seems to be a...Falling-Through-The-Air, Side-Kick-Twist-Flip?

Which sounds amazing on paper, but in reality is a blur of waving limbs.

He hits the trampoline with a heavy creak of springs and an "OOF!" then bounces back into the air, arms flailing and eyes wide, and lands on his face.

I do my best not to laugh and fail. Miserably.

He quickly gets up, and I notice with surprise that Robert is smiling. Sure, it looks like he hasn't smiled in quite some time (say, 300 years), but it is still a smile.

"How'd that go?" I try to keep a straight face. "And what in the world was all that...flailing?"

Robert brushes off his black combat pants. "Oh, that was all part of the effect. It was alright, but I was anticipating more of a challenge."

I notice one of his eyes is swelling. "What's going on with your eye? It's looking kinda... pink."

He stiffens. "Pink? Seriously, pink? Are you kidding me!?" He raises a hand to his face. "Err, I must've accidentally hit it. Didn't even notice."

I shrug. "If you say so. You wanna go again?"

Robert yawns. "As much as I'd like to, I have somewhere to be. Also, it's pretty obvious this hasn't got anything to do with Extreme Wilderness Survival or Land Creature Defense. I was expecting something...deadlier."

In our few brief previous encounters, which had involved Robert hitting me with a stick and pushing me into a mud pit, he had mentioned this stuff a couple times, and I'd assumed they were part of some some weird Boy Scout program.

But now I'm not so sure.

For the first time I wonder who this boy is. Where does he live? Is he homeschooled like me, which could explain why he's always playing around in the woods? And what the heck is a Bog Creep? I turn, wanting answers.

But Robert has disappeared into the deep shadows of the trees.

I wonder when we'll meet again—and if I should wear armor so I'll be ready.

∼

THANKS FOR READING THE PENCIL KILLER AND INTO THIN AIR.

If you're wondering what to read next, it's probably time for a full-length Casey Grimes novel. Learn more at **ajvanderhorst.com**.

For all the inside stuff on the Casey Grimes universe—including a free story, book news, and tips on fighting monsters—sign up for *The Sylvan Spy* at **ajvanderhorst.com/invisible.**

About the Authors

Asher Vanderhorst is an acclaimed cartoonist and emerging author. He also enjoys overly-sugary drinks. This is Asher's first published story. Check out his twice-a-week webtoon at **b.link/Asher**

Aidan Vanderhorst is a custom shoe creator and basketball player who makes a mean cappuccino. This is Aidan's two-hundred and seventeenth tall tale, but the first one he has written down. Check out his shoe designs at **b.link/Aidan**

AJ Vanderhorst is Aidan and Asher's dad. He's also author of the award-winning Casey Grimes books. If you're interested in secret forest societies, tree fortresses and monster control, learn more at **ajvanderhorst.com**.

THE END

READY TO READ A FREE STORY, PICK A NEW T-SHIRT, OR JOIN A SECRET MESSAGE RING?

HEAD OVER TO AJVANDERHORST.COM